TWEETY AND
SYLVESTER

TWEETY
and
SYLVESTER
THE MAGIC VOICE

by

Laura French

and

Rita Ritchie

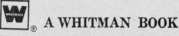 A WHITMAN BOOK

Western Publishing Company, Inc.

Racine, Wisconsin

CONTENTS

A Happy Tweety

CHAPTER 1

THE MAGIC VOICE

"Chirp, *twitter*, TWEET!"

Sylvester the cat held his paws over his ears. "What's got into Tweety, that crooning canary? He's been warbling his little head off for the last couple of days. Hey, bird-brain, turn off the tunes—or you'll be singing from inside a luscious

Tweety-bird sandwich!"

Tweety stopped swinging in his cage. "Uh-oh! I tawt I heard a vewy cwabby Puddy Tat. *Do, re, mi—*"

"Cut out that racket!" Sylvester jumped up and pounded the cage.

"Help! I'm getting dizzy!" Tweety cried as the cage jiggled wildly.

"*Sylvester!*" Granny scolded as she entered the room. "Stop bothering Tweety! Shame on you!"

"Poor little Tweety," sang Tweety.

Granny opened her pocketbook.

"Cut Out That Racket!"

"Sylvester, please go to the store and buy a big box of Aria birdseed. That's what makes Tweety sing so prettily. He picked it out all by himself a week ago."

Sylvester took the money and left the house. "A new brand of birdseed? Nonstop singing? That canary's trying to improve his pipes. But why?"

Sylvester bought the birdseed and started for home, still puzzling over Tweety's new ambition. "He's up to something. I wish I could figure out *what!*"

"Go to the Store."

Just then a gust of wind blew a printed leaflet into Sylvester's face. He started to throw it away, but some of the words caught his eye.

"Sufferin' succotash! It's a singing contest! And first prize is a trip around the world. Wow!" Light dawned suddenly. "So that's what Tweety's up to. He's eating special stuff and practicing his chirping because he wants to win that prize. I'll show him! We cats are great singers. I may be a little rusty, of course. *Ahem, cough, cough.*" He leaned against a building and took

"It's a Singing Contest!"

a deep breath. "O, solo mee-oow!"

Three stories above Sylvester, in a scientific laboratory, two men were having a serious talk.

"We must destroy my new invention, Higby, and we must do it at once!"

"But, Professor Branepan, you'd be throwing away two years' work! Besides, your new chemical will make you a rich man."

"True, Higby. But after all our tests, I have decided that my Magic Voice capsules could be dangerous if they got into the hands

Discussing an Invention

of someone evil—or incredibly stupid."

"But think of all the good they will do, Professor!" Higby said. A person getting a whiff of the Magic Voice vapor will immediately have an enchantingly beautiful voice—at least until the effect wears off.

"With the help of Magic Voice, teachers will be so pleasant to listen to that children will learn faster. And everyone will talk so agreeably that nobody will ever get angry at anybody. Workers,

Higby Protests

housewives, students—all will like
what they hear when someone
speaks using Magic Voice!"

Professor Branepan sighed.
"That's the very danger, Higby!
Imagine a dishonest salesman
talking people out of their life's
savings that easily. Think of bad
people persuading good ones to do
something that is terribly wrong!

"Worst of all, an unscrupulous
politician could use Magic Voice to
get to be head of our country. He
could become a dictator, making
people actually *like* listening to

"That's the Danger!"

his orders. We would all be his willing slaves, Higby! I cannot let that happen! We must destroy all my records and all samples of Magic Voice in this laboratory."

Higby nodded sadly. "You are right, Professor Branepan. We can start as soon as that new assistant janitor leaves the laboratory."

Over in the corner, the assistant janitor pretended to be sweeping while he eavesdropped on the two scientists. *It's lucky I wangled this job*, he thought. *I knew I'd find some secret worth stealing from*

Alaric Degoth, Industrial Spy

*the famous Professor Branepan.
Let them destroy the invention! I'll
take the vial of Magic Voice
capsules I've hidden behind the
window curtain, and I'll have them
analyzed so I can sell the formula.
Then I, Alaric Degoth, industrial
spy, will be rich!*

Professor Branepan approached
him. "You can leave now, Al. We
have some work to do here."

"Yes, sir. I'll finish up tonight,"
Alaric Degoth replied, putting
down his broom. *Tonight,* he
thought, *I'll return for the vial of*

"You Can Leave Now."

Magic Voice capsules!

Into the lab, from somewhere outside, came the screeching of a cat. "What a racket!" exclaimed the professor. "Close the window, Higby!"

Higby hurried to the window. "Oops! Something fell out—a test tube, I think."

"Never mind. Let's go to work."

In the street below, Sylvester cleared his throat. "I was rustier than I thought. But with a little practice, I— What's that?"

A glass vial fell on his foot. The

"Oops! Something Fell."

cap popped off, and a little capsule struck the sidewalk. *Poof!* The capsule turned into a vapor that quickly disappeared as Sylvester bent over to pick up the vial. "Funny cloud," he said to himself as he put the cap back on the vial of capsules. "*Aachoo!* Huh, sneezy stuff! Well, back to practice. *Do, re, mi.* . . ." To his surprise, he hit a beautiful high note. "Leapin' catfish!" he marveled. "It's all coming back to me now!" He hit the note again.

"There he is, gang! Our favorite

"Funny Cloud."

singer—Frankie Feline! After him, girls!"

Half a dozen young cats came running toward Sylvester. "I saw him first!" "No, he's mine!" "Oh, let me touch him!"

Sylvester cringed before the onslaught. "Sufferin' succotash! Feet, get going!"

The latest singing idol tore down the street, hotly pursued by a pack of wild young fans.

"Our Favorite Singer!"

Limping Home

CHAPTER 2

SYLVESTER'S SECRET

Sylvester limped toward Granny's house. He was covered with bruises and scratches from his young admirers' snatching pieces of his fur for souvenirs before he could escape.

"Funny—I never sang that well before. All I did was sneeze and—"

Then he remembered the vial still clutched in his paw. He read the label: *Magic Voice. Take as needed.* "Needed for what? I wonder."

Sylvester paused in thought. Finally he figured it out. "I get it! It's a kind of cat birdseed. It gives you a great new voice! Mee-rrroo-oowerrrr. . . ." Sylvester's voice ran up the scale, ending on a high, screeching note.

Clunk! A shoe dropped down on his head, and someone yelled, "Shoo, cat, shoo!"

"*Ulp!* I'm back to my normal

Reading the Label

voice. Guess this magic stuff wears off after a while." Then a crafty thought sneaked into his mind. "But it'll last long enough to win the singing contest. That ought to show Tweety up!"

When Sylvester got home, Granny was tapping her foot impatiently. "Sylvester, you've been fighting with Butch the dog again. Shame!"

"Tweety's hungwy for his birdseed," warbled the canary.

"I have your birdseed right—" Sylvester looked at his paws and

"You've Been Fighting!"

saw only the vial of Magic Voice. "Sufferin' succotash! I must've lost the box in the chase."

"Naughty Sylvester!" scolded Granny. "You go right to bed. I'll get Tweety's birdseed myself." She put on her hat and went out.

Tweety swung back and forth on his swing. *"Do, re, mi—"*

"Go ahead and practice, smarty," Sylvester told him. "I found out about that singing contest. You know who's going to win? Me, that's who!" He stomped off to his bed and settled down, glad to rest

Sylvester Makes a Promise

his aching bones. Soon he was snoring, even in sleep clutching the glass vial tightly.

"What makes Puddy Tat so sure he'll win the contest?" Tweety spied the vial in Sylvester's paw and zoomed in for a look. "Mm, *Magic Voice. Take as needed.* Needed for what? My little bwain is cwanking fuwiously."

In much less time than it had taken Sylvester, Tweety figured it out. "Oho! By some modern chemical discovery, my old and twusted fwiend is about to cheat in that

Spying the Vial

singing contest. Don't worry, Puddy. I'll save you from your worst self."

Tweety tugged at the vial in Sylvester's paw, but the cat just snorted in his sleep and rolled over, the paw holding the Magic Voice tucked safely under him.

"Never mind, Puddy. Tweety will watch his chance at the singing contest."

On contest day, Granny fed Tweety an extra portion of the special birdseed. Then she put on her best hat and picked up the cage.

Pulling Hard

"Come, Sylvester. We're going to listen to our Tweety sing in the contest."

"Yes, Granny." Sylvester smiled innocently. Little did Granny suspect that he was the one who would win the prize!

Backstage at the theater, they stood near the end of a long line, waiting to be called. At long last, it was their turn. Tweety said, "You go first, old fwiend, so I can appwaud for you."

"Okay." Sylvester put a paw in the vial and sneaked out one of

Waiting in Line

the Magic Voice capsules. Before
he could do anything with it,
Tweety dived at him and snatched
it out of his paw.

"Leapin' catfish! Tweety, come
back! Gimme my—er, uh—vitamins!" He grabbed for the canary.
Tweety chirped with laughter as he
circled overhead, out of reach.

Granny ordered, "Sylvester, you
stop that. Bad cat!"

"Bad tat!" chortled Tweety.

Enraged, Sylvester slashed with
his claws, snagging a couple of
yellow feathers.

"Gimme My—Er, Uh—Vitamins!"

Startled, Tweety dropped the capsule near Granny. The *poof!* was followed by Granny's sneeze.

Sylvester bounded after the canary. "I'll get you for this!"

"Goodness me!" cried Granny. "Sylvester! Tweety!" She ran after the cat and the canary. Her voice trilled sweetly as she called for them to stop. Through the backdrop, across the stage, and over the grand piano zoomed Tweety, chirping excitedly. Sylvester was just behind him, yowling and hissing.

As Granny ran after them both,

Granny Sneezes

begging them to behave, her words soared into a breathtaking melody.

Sylvester chased Tweety past the judges' table, where one of them reached out an arm and grabbed Sylvester by the scruff of the neck. "Quiet, you noisy feline!" he snapped. "You're drowning out those beautiful voices!" He carried Sylvester to the door and deposited him in the hallway. The judge went back inside, and Sylvester heard the key turn in the lock.

"That sneaky canary!" Sylvester said angrily. "He just cost me a

An Angry Judge

trip around the world. Well, I'll give him a trip—past my tonsils, with two slices of bread and some lettuce for luggage!"

Back onstage, Tweety sighed with relief when he saw Sylvester carried to the door. He flew back to Granny and perched on her shoulder, singing happily.

Granny crooned soothing words to her tiny pet. "Good little Tweety! The danger is past. Now you're safe at last. No pussycats near—you've nothing to fear."

The Magic Voice made the duet

A Beautiful Duet

absolutely beautiful. The audience
began clapping and shouting,
"Bravo! Bravo!"

Meanwhile, outside the theater,
Alaric Degoth, fake janitor and
genuine spy, trudged sadly along
the street. "I'm ruined," he moaned.
"I know the capsules were behind
the curtain when I left the lab, but
when I went back last night, they
were gone! Professor Branepan
and his assistant must have found
the vial and destroyed it, like they
destroyed all the rest of the stuff."
He dried a tear, then stopped in

A Dejected Alaric

amazement. "Listen! What a wonderful voice! Could it be? No! Yes!
It just might be!" He rushed into
the theater and saw the announcer
standing onstage with Granny and
Tweety.

"We have a winner in our singing contest," the announcer was
saying. "Or rather, we have *two*
winners: Granny and Tweety win
a trip around the world for their
duet, which was so beautiful that
not even a yowling tomcat could
spoil it!"

The audience cheered and

The Winners!

clapped. Alaric Degoth was stunned. "There's only one way the old gal could sing that well. Somehow, she got hold of the Magic Voice capsules. I'll have to get them back from her!"

Alaric Is Stunned

"Hi, Puddy Tat!"

CHAPTER 3

CAPTIVE CAT

Tweety flew along the corridors of the S.S. *Holiday*. Reaching the hold of the cruiser, he went in. Among the boxes and trunks, he found the little cage in which Sylvester was kept.

"Hi, Puddy Tat! Isn't this a swell voyage? Aren't you glad I talked Gwanny into letting you come along—even though *you* didn't win the contest?"

Sylvester grabbed two of the cage bars and shook them. "Tweety, you've got to get me out of here! I've been locked up for a week like —like some kind of animal!"

"Er, Gwanny and I twied hard, Puddy, but the captain won't change the rules. All pets aboard the ship have to be in cages."

"What about you?"

"I'm not a pet. I'm a contest winner!" Tweety told him. "Welax,

"Get Me Out of Here!"

Puddy Tat! In a week we'll be in Fwance. Then you can get out of your cage."

Sylvester sulked in a corner. "Why couldn't we fly across the ocean instead of sailing?" He added bitterly, "*You* have a private state-room. *You* go to the movies. *You* play shuffleboard and get in on all the lifeboat drills!"

Then he flung himself on his knees, begging. "Tell the captain I'll be good. I promise I won't get in the way! I'll even wear a collar and leash! Just give me a couple of

"I'll Be Good."

days out of this rotten cage!"

"Vewy well. I will see him soon at the Captain's Dinner," Tweety said. "We're having clam chowder, baked haddock, lobster. . . ." He recited a list of seafood that left Sylvester drooling. "I will come and tell you all about it," he promised, flying away. "Bye-bye!"

As Tweety flew to the dining room, he didn't notice a suspicious-looking deckhand lurking quietly in the shadows. Alaric Degoth had seen the prizewinners' itinerary in the local newspaper and had signed

Tweety Flies Away

on as a crew member on the S.S. *Holiday.*

A whole week on this rusty tub, he thought, and I still haven't found the Magic Voice capsules. They aren't in the old gal's luggage, and they aren't in the canary's cage. They must be hidden in the cat's cage—and that bird just led me right to him! Fame and fortune, here I come!

As Sylvester lay disconsolately in his cage, a man came up and said, "Hello, little kitty! My, you look sad. Can I help you?"

"Hello, Little Kitty!"

Hope sprang in Sylvester's heart. "Why, uh, sure, chum. How about taking the nice little kitty for a nice little walk around deck?"

"Glad to." Picking up the cage, Alaric walked out of the hold.

Sylvester said, "Uh, chum, I had more in mind you letting me out for a leisurely stroll."

"It's better to wait until dark so the sailors won't catch you," Alaric said. "Meanwhile, you can stay in my cabin, and I'll bring you tidbits from the Captain's Dinner."

"Better yet, could you smuggle

Carrying the Cage

me into the dining room?"

"Maybe later," Alaric said.

Suddenly the ship tilted sharply. The cage slipped from Alaric's hand, struck the deck, and sprang wide open.

Sylvester leaped out. "Free at last!" he shouted and dashed down the deck.

"Wait!" cried Alaric, running after him. He had nearly caught up, when Sylvester grabbed a stanchion and then swung up and over him.

"Never mind, chum. I'll find

"Free at Last!"

my own way to the dinner."
Sylvester sped gleefully down the
ship's deck.

Behind him, the man shouted,
"Sailors, catch that cat!"

Sylvester fled for all of his nine
lives as the man and two sailors
pounded after him. Funny how the
nice stranger had turned on him
like that!

Diving through some swinging
doors, Sylvester found himself in
the dining room just as dinner
started. He paused, sniffing. "Mm,
delicious! Maybe I could hide under

"Catch That Cat!"

Granny's table while Tweety slips me some delectable morsels."

"There he is!" yelled one of the pursuing sailors.

Sylvester took off once more. Women screamed, and men made wild grabs as the cat took to the tabletops, splashing through clam chowder, slowing slightly as he waded into a vast pan of jellied crab. The three men waded right after him.

"Catch that wild beast!" roared the furious captain.

One of the waiters grabbed a

Making a Mess

bowl of spiced apples and started
throwing them. Sylvester ducked,
then retaliated with gobs of caviar.

Ducking and weaving, the com-
batants carried their guerrilla war
down the long table, squishing
through pâté de foie gras, skidding
on lemon wedges. A sailor pelted
Sylvester with stuffed olives, and
the cat responded by shooting peas
out of celery sticks.

Then, in a sneak attack, a hand
reached out and grabbed Sylvester!

"I've got him!" cried Alaric.
"I'll lock him up in my cabin!"

A Food Fight

Sylvester's claws tore through the carpeting as the man dragged him away. "HELP! Granny! Tweety!"

"You leave my dear little pet alone, you brute!" cried Granny, running after them. She grabbed her pocketbook and began swinging at his head.

"Cut it out, lady!" Alaric Degoth dropped Sylvester and raised his arms to protect himself from the blows that rained down on his head.

"Throw this man in the brig!"

Granny to the Rescue

the captain ordered. "And don't let him out till we get to France!"

Alaric Degoth, former deckhand and failed catsnatcher, was led away by two husky sailors.

The captain turned to Sylvester. "And as for you, you—you meal wrecker!"

Sylvester shook as he faced the captain, whose white uniform was splotched with jellied crab, caviar, and squashed peas. A wilted lettuce leaf hung over one ear.

"I ought to make you walk the plank! Because of you, my dinner

"You—You Meal Wrecker!"

is spoiled and I've lost one good deckhand!"

Tweety chirped, "Captain, I have an idea...." He whispered in the captain's ear.

The captain smiled and nodded. Then he bowed to Granny. "Now, madam, may I escort you back to dinner?"

After they had left, Sylvester asked, "Tweety, what did you say to the captain?"

"I only told him of a way you could spend the west of the cwuise out on deck."

Offering a Suggestion

"Say, thanks, pal!"

Suddenly a sailor grabbed Sylvester and shoved a pail and a mop into his paws. "Start working, cat! Captain's orders!"

"Cheer up, Puddy," said Tweety as Sylvester reluctantly began scrubbing the deck under the watchful eye of the sailor. "It's only for one more week!"

Mopping the Decks

Chasing Tweety

CHAPTER 4

BALLOON ANTICS

Seven days later, the trio of
tourists arrived in Paris and
checked into their hotel.

Sylvester immediately did two
things to recover from his brief
and tiring career as a deckhand.

First, he chased Tweety six
times around the room before

Granny could stop him.

Then he took a long, hot shower, and with the help of one of the Magic Voice capsules he carried with him, he sang and scrubbed away his bad mood.

Sylvester's clear, lovely notes drifted into the next room, where they found an extremely interested listener.

"That sounds like that ornery cat," said Alaric Degoth, who had caught up with the trio after his release from the brig. "And he must still have the Magic Voice

Singing in the Shower

capsules. I'll have to stay close
and wait for my next chance to
nab him."

The very next morning, Degoth
was sitting on his balcony, pre-
tending to read a newspaper while
Granny and her two pets stood
looking out over the city.

"They're sure giving us the
red-carpet treatment," said
Sylvester.

"It's all planned in advance,"
said Granny, "everything we do
and see in each country on our
trip. This morning we're going

Making Plans

to the balloon race. And we'd
better hurry or we'll be late."

From behind a potted palm,
Alaric Degoth watched them leave.
As soon as they were gone, he
let himself into their room and
went through their luggage.

But Alaric's search was for
nothing. The Magic Voice vial was
not in their hotel room. "That
crafty cat must have taken it
with him."

Rushing out of the hotel, he
hailed a taxi. Inside, he put on
a fake beard and glasses.

Alaric Watches

Tweety, Sylvester, and Granny got to the race as the first hot-air balloon sailed into the sky. The crowd cheered. Tweety hopped up and down. "I wish I could go for a ride in a balloon!"

"I'm going to get us some ice cream," Granny said. "Sylvester, hold my camera case until I get back."

As Tweety and Sylvester stood waiting for Granny, a man with a bushy beard and glasses came up to them. His beady eyes gleamed when he saw the leather case

A Balloon Race

Sylvester was holding. "I see zat Monsieur Cat has the American camera. I am *très* interested in cameras. May I see?" He grabbed eagerly for the case.

"I don't think I twust that man," Tweety muttered suspiciously. He snatched the camera case and flew away.

"Come back here, you flying piece of lunch meat!" Sylvester cried.

"We have to get wid of Mr. Bushy Beard," Tweety explained. "Get into this balloon!"

"Come Back Here!"

Sylvester jumped into the basket. Tweety started to turn valves, pull levers, and cast off ropes. The balloon suddenly bounded up. "Hooway, we're flying!" cried Tweety.

"Sufferin' succotash!" Sylvester felt butterflies in his stomach as the crowd below grew smaller. "You featherbrain, we're in the balloon race!"

"So is Mr. Bushy Beard," Tweety said, gazing below. "He got into balloon number eleven."

Sylvester bit his nails. "Wish

Airborne!

we could turn this windbag
around."

"Number eleven is gaining,"
said Tweety. "I'll dump some
sand."

He pulled a rope, and two sand-
bags dropped away. The balloon
bounced higher.

"You mean *you* can fly this
thing?" asked Sylvester, stunned.

"They tell all about it in that
gweat TV series, *Lieutenant
Beaky and His Balloononauts*."

Sylvester leaned over the edge
of the basket. "Tweety, number

A Balloon Chase

eleven is faster'n us. The crook
is right below. Now he's coming
up— *Oops!*"

Sylvester suddenly slipped over
the edge. Frantically he clawed
at the ropes hanging there.
"TWEETY!"

"Hang on, Puddy!" Tweety
rushed up just as Sylvester's grip
failed. Down, down he fell, landing *smack* on top of number
eleven, which was rapidly rising
to the height of their balloon!

Up, up went Sylvester on top
of number eleven, until he was

"TWEETY!"

level with the basket from which
he had fallen.

Tweety shouted, "Jump,
Puddy!"

Sylvester squeezed his eyes shut.
"I-I can't." He floated up out of
reach as number eleven rose still
higher.

When the baskets of both bal-
loons were momentarily even,
Alaric Degoth suddenly grabbed
the ropes and swung over into
Tweety's basket. "Aha! Now I
will have it!"

"I will fight to the death,"

Grabbing the Rope

cried Tweety bravely.

On top of number **eleven**, Sylvester peeked out from behind a paw as he soared past Tweety and Bushy Beard in the other balloon. Above him—thin air. Below—solid city.

"S-Sufferin' succotash! Stuck on a runaway windbag, with nobody to steer! B-Better jump." He took a deep breath and leaped off the balloon.

Thump! He landed on the bag of Tweety's balloon. He began sliding down the curved surface.

"B-Better Jump."

Frantically Sylvester dug in his claws to stop.

Sssssssssssssss!

"Sheesh, the air's getting warm all of a sudden." An instant later, he realized what had happened. "Tweety, the b-balloon's collapsing!"

Tweety was fluttering protectively over Granny's camera case on the floor of the basket. "Keep away, you cwook! Doodness, are we falling?"

Alaric gave up his attempt to seize the case and rushed to the

A Punctured Balloon

edge of the basket. The city rapidly came closer as the hot air went out of the balloon.

From above came Sylvester's wail: "Tweeeety, stop this thing! I want to get off!"

"Look out!" cried Alaric. "The Eiffel Tower—we're going to hit!"

Crunch! The sagging balloon folded over the top of the tower. A door below them popped open and a man shouted up. "Monsieurs, it is not permitted to tether the balloon to the Eiffel Tower!"

Alaric Degoth scrambled down

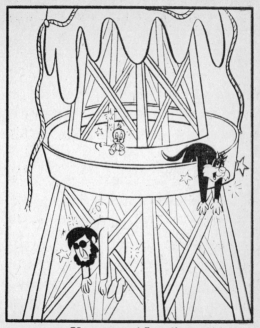

Unexpected Landing

to the door, Granny's camera case in his hands. Tweety flew after him, shouting, "Stop, thief!"

Sylvester slid down cautiously. When he entered the observation platform, he found Tweety, alone with the camera case, gathering up all the rolls of film and spare lenses that had spilled from it. "Looks like Bushy Beard got away," said Sylvester. "But your quick thinking saved Granny's camera. Thanks, little bud—"

A hand clamped on his shoulder. Sylvester looked up into the face

Gathering Equipment

of a French policeman and tried to grin.

The *gendarme* looked stern. "Monsieur Le Chat, you take this balloon without permission, you fly it without the license, you land on the Eiffel Tower—"

"Not me, Your Honor," said Sylvester. "This crazy canary did all that. I just went along for the ride."

"... *and* you kidnap the canary," finished the *gendarme*. "Fly away, little canary. You are safe now."

Tweety chirped innocently as

A Stern *Gendarme*

the policeman marched Sylvester away. "Don't worry, Puddy Tat. I'll tell Gwanny all about it so she can bail you out—in two or three days."

Under Arrest

A Gliding Gondola

CHAPTER 5

STARS FOR A DAY

A week had passed, and the happy travelers had left their Paris problems behind them. They were enjoying Italy.

"Venice is full of boats," said Tweety. From the bank of a canal, they watched gondolas being rowed through the waterway.

"People use them instead of cars."

"You would, too, if your streets were flooded all the time," said Sylvester. "Let's go for a ride."

Soon they were riding in a gondola through one of Venice's many canals. Tweety strained and struggled with the single long oar while Sylvester lounged in the bow.

When they came to an intersection, Sylvester said, "Turn left."

Instead, the gondola began to go to the right. "Let's go this way, Puddy Tat," Tweety said.

"Left!" Sylvester walked back

Sylvester Relaxes

and stood over the canary.

Tweety flourished his pole. "I say wight!"

Sylvester grabbed at Tweety's oar. Unexpectedly, the canary pushed it. Sylvester yelled, "Look out!" and fell to the bottom of the gondola. His little glass Magic Voice vial rolled out and popped open. A capsule struck the side of the gondola and instantly vaporized, *poof!* Sylvester sneezed. Tweety sneezed.

The cat recovered the vial. "You almost made me lose this, you bird-

Sneezing Companions

brain!" he exclaimed.

His words were harsh, but the effects of Magic Voice made them sound so pleasant that Tweety wasn't upset.

"I'm sowwy, Puddy Tat," he said. "Let's compwomise and go stwaight ahead. Wemember, we have to get back to Gwanny in time to go to the opewa."

Tweety, too, had inhaled Magic Voice, and Sylvester immediately forgot to be angry.

"I wouldn't miss it," said Sylvester. *"Puss in Boots* is all

Pleasant Sounds

about the adventures of a great
and handsome cat."

"And how his birdie fwiend
gets him out of scwapes," added
Tweety. He raised his voice in
song. "If my furry pal gets in
twouble, I fly to his aid on the
double."

Sylvester's voice soared over
the water. "He tries to help, but
in the end, I have to rescue my
feathered friend."

A few blocks away, Alaric
Degoth searched frantically
through the crooked streets.

Soaring Voices

"Where is that cat? He and the canary are sitting ducks, out in a gondola on these deserted canals, and I have to lose them! But I'll get them, and when I do, I'll force that dumb cat to give me the Magic Voice."

He paused. "Just think—with those capsules, everyone will do just what I say. I'll have wealth, power!" He blinked. "I hear singing! It must be—" He rushed to the canal bank and saw Tweety and Sylvester sharing an oar and singing a marvelous duet.

"I Hear Singing!"

Alaric whispered, "The Magic Voice—they have it with them! And all I have to do is catch them! Quick, where's a gondola?"

Meanwhile, in an office building beside the canal, the great opera impresario D.C. Fine paced back and forth. "Call the hospital again, Giuseppe. See if Adagio and Scherzo have recovered."

Giuseppe made the call, then shook his head. "Sorry, D.C.; their voices still have not come back. I tell you, maestro, those roles are impossible to sing!"

A Worried Impresario

D.C. flung out his hands. "And that's the problem! The matinee of *Puss in Boots* starts in one hour, and no one else can perform those roles! What am I to do, Giuseppe?"

Suddenly Giuseppe stepped to the open window. "Listen, D.C.!"

Two wonderful voices, entwined in a duet, came through the window. D.C. Fine cried, "What magnificent harmony! I thought I knew every singer in Italy. Who are they?" He looked out and gasped in astonishment.

"Listen!"

"*Sforzando!* A real cat and a real canary—with voices like angels! Er, Giuseppe. . . ."

His assistant smiled. "Our matinee goes on as scheduled, D.C.!"

Tweety and Sylvester, carried away by their own singing, let the gondola drift as their improvised duet floated among the old walls of Venice.

D.C. Fine stuck his head out the window. "Gentlemen!" he called to Tweety and Sylvester. "How would you two like to be rich and famous?"

"Gentlemen!"

"Sure!" said Sylvester immediately. "What did you have in mind?"

"It's nothing dishonest, I twust," Tweety added cautiously.

D.C. Fine laughed. "No, no, it is a thing of great honor! We need someone to sing the lead roles in the opera this afternoon."

"The opewa? Oh, goody!" chirped Tweety.

"Just give us a minute to park this floating flivver, and we'll be right up," Sylvester promised.

Only a few yards behind them,

A Sensational Offer

Alaric Degoth groaned in dismay.
"The opera! That means reporters!
The secret of Magic Voice will be
out, and so will I—out of a fortune! I have to stop those two!"

Inside the opera house, D.C.
Fine greeted Tweety and Sylvester
warmly. "There is not much time.
You must go now and get into
your costumes. While you are gone,
I will prepare your new contract
with the opera company. You will
be wealthy!"

Alaric Degoth pretended to tune
a piano while he listened to D.C.

"You Will Be Wealthy!"

Fine's promises. "What can I do?" he mumbled. "If I try to make off with the cat now, Fine'll have every policeman in Italy on my trail. I've got it! I'll make D.C. Fine himself get rid of those two!"

He followed the maestro to his office and burst through the door.

"Good day, Mr. Fine. I'm Tweety and Sylvester's agent. They have a few requests to make for their new contract."

"Of course, sir, anything within reason," the maestro answered.

"Very well. Private dressing

"I'm Their Agent."

rooms, of course. Chauffeured lim-
ousines—one apiece. Six months of
paid vacation. Time and a half for
curtain calls—"

"What?" shrieked D.C. Fine.
"Those ingrates! I plucked them
from the canal and offered them
stardom, and this is how they
treat me! Out! *Out!*" He shoved
Alaric Degoth through the door
and slammed it behind him.
Degoth smiled and faded into the
shadows.

A few moments later, Tweety
and Sylvester walked proudly into

"Those Ingrates!"

D.C. Fine's office.

"Here we are, your maestro-ship," proclaimed Sylvester. "Your new stars!"

"Stars!" D.C. Fine snorted. "I would not hire you two to sell popcorn during intermission! I will refund the ticket money. The performance is cancelled! Get out of my sight!"

Sylvester and Tweety walked slowly along the bank of the canal.

"Poor Gwanny," said Tweety. "Now she won't see the opewa."

"Get Out!"

"Was it something I said?" Sylvester asked sadly.

"Cheer up, Puddy Tat," Tweety told him. "You may not be wich and famous, but you still have me!"

"Yeah," Sylvester agreed, his eyes beginning to gleam. "And that reminds me—I haven't had lunch!" Sylvester pounced, but Tweety stayed one jump ahead of him—all the way to the hotel.

Sylvester Is Hungry

The Castle Slough

CHAPTER 6

THE GHOST OF LOCH MESS

"Leapin' catfish, look at that creepy castle!" Sylvester shivered as the taxi bore him, Tweety, and Granny to the place where they were to stay in Scotland.

Granny said, "My, we certainly are lucky to be staying here! This famous castle takes only two or

151

three paying guests at a time."

Inside the castle's great hall, a man greeted them. "Good day, madam. I'm Angus Fitzenstarts, present owner of Castle Slough here on the shores of Loch Mess. Tonight is the one time of the year when our resident ghost, heh-heh, is supposed to walk. Perhaps you will be fortunate enough to see him during the night."

Suddenly the visor of a nearby suit of armor clanged shut.

"Sheesh! He's here already!" cried a scared Sylvester, leaping

A Great Hall

for the nearest doorway.

"No, no, Puddy!" said Tweety, flying after him. "That was just me, checking for dust."

"How about checking on your empty head?" said Sylvester, taking a swipe at him with his paw.

"Sylvester, leave Tweety alone!" scolded Granny.

Angus Fitzenstarts broke in. "There is just time for a late supper before you retire for the night." He snapped his fingers. "Duff, show our three guests to their rooms."

"Show Our Guests Their Rooms."

Tweety looked closely at the servant. "Haven't I seen you some-place before?"

"Whaddaya mean—er, that is, hoot mon, nae!" He picked up their suitcases. "This way, lady and gentlemen." The servant led them upstairs and down a hall. "Here's Madam's room."

Granny opened the door. "See you later, boys. Do behave."

"We will!" chorused Tweety and Sylvester.

They followed Duff down the long hall, up some back stairs,

"Here's Madam's Room."

and through another long corridor before at last opening the door to their room.

"How do we find our way down to supper?" Sylvester asked. "That is, if I don't decide to have a Tweety-bird feast!"

"Supper will be brought to your room, sorr," said Duff.

By the time they had unpacked, Duff was back with a cart of food. After they had eaten, Sylvester yawned and stretched. "Time to hit the hay. Tomorrow I'll go fishing in Loch Mess."

A Tired Cat

Tweety snuggled down in his cage, which Duff had hung up. Soon he and Sylvester were fast asleep and snoring.

Late that night, someone shook Sylvester awake. "Wake up, sorr! 'Tis me, Duff." He held a candle.

"Wazza matter?" Sylvester rubbed sleepy eyes.

Duff said, "The old gal—er, Madam woke up with a nightmare. She wants to see you."

Tweety blinked his eyes. "I tawt I taw a candle. Turn the lights on, Mr. Duff."

"Wake Up, Sorr!"

"The fuses blew out. Come on, I'll show you to the old gal—er, to Madam's room."

It was very dark in the hall as Tweety and Sylvester followed Duff. The flickering candle made spooky shadows move along the old walls.

"C-Creeps, I hope Duff knows the way," quavered Sylvester.

"Don't worry, Puddy," comforted Tweety. "You can hold my wing."

Empty suits of armor looked as if they were moving as the three

Duff Leads the Way

walked past with the candle. Big shadows lurked in the corners. They went downstairs, along more halls, down other stairs.

Sylvester swallowed nervously. "How about our calling it a night and all of us going back to our own rooms?"

"Just a bit farther, sorr," said Duff reassuringly. His candle was burning low.

Tweety flew up to inspect the walls they passed. "Mmm, I tawt I taw dwipping-wet bwicks and a big spider web," he muttered to

"Just a Bit Farther."

himself. "I don't twust Mr. Duff.
These unused chambers are full of
boxes and old wags. They give me
an idea."

Quickly Tweety put a cloth bun-
dle under one wing. Then he hurried down the dark and damp
corridor to catch up. "Sylvester!
Mr. Duff!"

His little voice was muffled by
the dank atmosphere.

Then he saw candlelight at the
bottom of another flight of stairs.
Swooping down to investigate,
Tweety saw Duff in a cell-like

"Sylvester! Mr. Duff!"

room, bending over the unconscious
Sylvester.

"Time for action," the canary
decided. Draping himself in the old
sheet he'd been carrying, he flew
waveringly in front of Duff.

"Hoooo-haa! Boooo . . . hoooo!"

"Help—it's the ghost!" cried
Duff. Leaping out of the chamber,
he slammed the huge iron door
behind him and shot the bolt.

"Yeeek!" screamed Sylvester as
he opened his eyes.

"It's only me, Puddy!" Tweety
pulled off the sheet. "But I'm

"It's the Ghost!"

afwaid we're locked in the castle dungeon. There's no way out."

"Aye, there is, laddies," said a friendly voice. A cheerful-looking little Scotsman stepped into the candlelight. "Follow me through yon secret passageway."

He pushed open a secret door and led Tweety and Sylvester through a maze of stairs and halls. Finally they were safely back in their room.

"That Duff laddie was looking for something you have," said the Scot. "A wicked fellow he is!"

"Follow Me, Laddies."

As their rescuer went off down the dark hall, Tweety thought he heard the faint echo of bagpipes playing.

When Tweety and Sylvester joined Granny for breakfast, Angus Fitzenstarts was showing her a painting. "This is old Sandy McSlough, whose ghost walks once a year. I think one of my servants must have seen him last night. I just hired Duff two days ago, but he has suddenly run away."

"That picture!" gasped Sylvester. "The nice guy last night—he

"That Picture!"

was the ghost!" *Klunk!* Sylvester fainted.

"Poor Puddy," said Tweety, "I guess the excitement of twavel just tires him out."

Sylvester Faints

Relaxing

CHAPTER 7

INTO THE BULLRING

"This is the life," sighed Tweety, swinging in the hammock inside his cage. "Lounging by a motel pool in Portugal while Gwanny goes shopping."

"And in a few minutes, we'll go right across the street to the bullring to see the great Gatorro,"

added Sylvester. "Just think—he's
the only pussycat bullfighter in the
world. I sure hope I can get his
autograph!"

"He must be there alweady,"
said Tweety, finishing his lemon-
ade. "The stands are getting
cwowded."

"Then let's get started! I want
to get a good seat."

Tweety and Sylvester walked to
the gates. Sylvester elbowed his
way impatiently through the
crowd, determined to get in before
the stands filled up.

Entering the Stadium

The people in the crowd turned to glare at the rude intruder, but as soon as they saw Sylvester, they moved out of the way. "It's Gatorro!" they murmured.

A man ran up to Sylvester. "Senhor Gatorro—at last! There is no time to lose. Come!" He rushed Sylvester down some stairs. Tweety flew after them.

In a small dressing room, the man and a helper quickly thrust Sylvester into a fancy bullfighter's costume. Then three other men entered dressed as picadors. They

"Senhor Gatorro—at Last!"

took Sylvester's arms. "Senhor Gatorro, our horses, the bull, and your public are waiting. Hurry!"

"Hey, wait a minute!"

Before Sylvester could explain, the men swept him off into the bullring. Tweety, hurrying to keep up, heard the door lock with a click behind him.

When "Gatorro" and his picadors entered the ring, a tremendous cheer rose from the crowd.

The men handed Sylvester a cape and then mounted their horses. A gate opened, and a bull trotted out.

"Wait a Minute!"

The picadors rode close, startling the bull and making him angry. The beast pawed the ground, then began to gallop right toward Sylvester, his eyes red with rage.

"Run, Puddy!" cried Tweety.

"M-My knees w-won't work!"

Nearer and nearer charged the bull, until Tweety could hear him snorting. "Flap the cape, Puddy!"

Somehow Sylvester made his arms move. The edge of the cape snapped against the bull's nose, and the huge animal veered away.

"It worked! Say, this isn't so

The Bull Charges

bad!" exclaimed Sylvester, suddenly cocky. "I could be another
Gatorro!"

"Start pwacticing," advised
Tweety. "Here he comes again."

Sylvester swung the cape, but
the bull only galloped faster. Frantically flapping the cape, Sylvester
jumped aside at the last moment,
and the bull thundered past.

"Boo! Coward!" yelled out the
angry crowd. "Where is Gatorro's
bravery?"

One of the picadors rode up.
"Senhor, we drive the bull toward

Waving the Cape

you. Are you not ready for him?"

"G-Gulp!" Sylvester shuddered. "I'll never be ready. Let me out!. I'm not Gatorro!"

"Many bullfighters get nervous now and then." The man rode off, then again drove the bull toward Sylvester.

Sylvester tried to scramble up the smooth wooden side of the ring, but it was too high. The ground shook as the bull galloped toward him. "Help, TWEETY!"

Tweety fluttered in alarm. "My doodness, where is Gatorro? I must

"Let Me Out!"

find him!" Off he flew.

In a parking lot behind the stands, Tweety saw a cat who looked just like Sylvester. The cat was tied hand and foot, and a familiar-looking bully was standing over him, shouting, "Where is it? Give me those capsules!"

When Alaric Degoth spied Tweety hovering nearby, he began to chuckle evilly. "So—it's you to the rescue again, eh? Well, birdie, this time you're too late! I have your friend, and I won't let him go until he tells me—"

A Startling Discovery

"No, sir!" cried Tweety. "That isn't my fwiend!"

"What?" asked Alaric Degoth.

"This is the gweat Gatorro! Sylvester is in the bullwing, fighting a mean and angwy bull. If you don't let this puddy tat go, *my* puddy tat will be twampled by those big, heavy hooves!"

"Trampled!" Degoth exclaimed. "Great greenbacks, he'll be killed!" *And the Magic Voice he's got with him will be destroyed*, he added to himself.

Degoth quickly untied the great

"That Isn't My Fwiend!"

Gatorro. "To the bullring!" he cried. "Let's go!"

When they reached the stands, Alaric shoved Gatorro toward the bullring.

"Not yet!" the bullfighter said haughtily. "First I must put on the costume of the matador!"

"What the— Oh, all right," Degoth said impatiently. "But hurry!"

Leaping into the ring, Alaric snatched the bullfighter's cape from Sylvester and flourished it in front of the bull. The huge beast

Racing Toward the Bullring

swerved aside, narrowly missing Sylvester, who was now groveling in the dirt.

"Run, you stupid cat!" Alaric snarled as the bull circled for another attack.

"The door's l-locked, your saviorship, sir," a frightened Sylvester quavered.

"Quick, give me the Mag— Oh, never mind!"

Alaric just had time to snap the cape in the bull's face as the angry beast thundered past. The spy's knees shook with fear, but the

"Run, You Stupid Cat!"

thought of losing the Magic Voice and his chance for power kept him from running. Each time the bull charged, he managed to wave it away with the cape. But he was tiring rapidly—and the unhappy fans were throwing pop bottles at him and Sylvester.

Suddenly a figure in a splendid bullfighter's costume rushed into the ring, directly in the bull's path. The real Gatorro stood there fearlessly as the bull came snorting and bellowing. Gatorro turned the beast away with an easy flick of

Gatorro to the Rescue

his cape. Alaric, out of sheer relief, fainted.

Tweety fluttered to Sylvester's ear. "The door's unlocked now. Let's go!"

Later, as they sat by the motel pool, Tweety asked Sylvester, "Did you notice anything stwange about that man who saved you fwom the bull today?"

"Frankly, chum, I was too busy to notice. Why?"

"I have a funny feeling I've seen him before," Tweety said. "And he acted vewy odd. When he thought

"Let's Go!"

Gatorro was you, he was vewy nasty. But when he knew *you* were you, he twied to save your life! Why do you think he did that?"

"Who cares?" replied Sylvester. "He *did* save my life, and that's all *I* care about. But I do wish I'd had a chance to thank him. It isn't every day that some stranger saves my life!"

"Hmm," Tweety mused. "Don't worry, Puddy Tat. I have a feeling we'll be seeing him again!"

Discussing the Stranger

The Great Pyramids

CHAPTER 8

MYSTERY MUMMY

"The pyramids took hundreds of years to build," said the guide as Granny marveled at the three great structures in the Egyptian desert.

"Did that include time out for lunch?" asked Sylvester. "Coffee breaks? Vacations?"

"I will take you inside now, but

you must stay close to me," warned the guide. "It is easy to get lost in these many winding passage-ways—dangerous, also."

"Heavenly days!" said Granny. "Sylvester, look after Tweety, now. I should think they'd hire more guides so people wouldn't be afraid of getting lost, Mr. Abdul."

"That is not easy, madam," said Abdul as he led them through a small doorway. "Only yesterday, one of our newly hired guides was fired because he was too nosy about the visitors to the pyramids. *Good*

Following the Guide

workers would rather be in Cairo, where the action is. This way, madam. Please watch your step."

Abdul led them down a long stone passage, pointing out some of its features. They went upstairs and down another hall. Then Abdul stopped before a group of figures painted on a wall. He began explaining what it meant. "And this is the sacred Egyptian cat. The ancients thought the cat brought them good luck, and they often buried many cats with their dead kings."

A Sacred Egyptian Cat

Tweety snickered. "Don't you wish that you were an Egyptian tat, Puddy?"

"If I were a royal cat, I'd live on Tweety-bird sandwiches!" Sylvester snarled.

Tweety and Sylvester were so busy taunting each other that they didn't notice a mummy that was propped against a wall of the passageway. This mummy was different from the others they'd seen: It had beady eyes that watched every move the cat and the canary made.

Watching Eyes

As soon as the tourists had passed, Alaric Degoth left his spot by the wall and hopped after them. *Drat this outfit*, he thought. *But since that canary saw me at the bullring, I have to be sure he doesn't recognize me. I'll just wait until those two get separated from the guide and the old gal, and then—*

Tweety stopped suddenly and spun around, and Alaric froze in his tracks.

"Uh-oh," said Tweety. "I tawt I taw that mummy move!"

The Mummy Follows

"Don't be such a birdbrain, birdbrain. That mummy's been dead for thousands of years," Sylvester told him. "Come on, let's get out of here."

The stone passage was deserted. Granny and the Egyptian guide had vanished.

"Now look what you've done!" Sylvester shouted. "Granny and the guide have turned off into one of the other tunnels! We're lost!"

Now's my chance, thought Alaric Degoth. He lunged at Sylvester.

"Yikes!" shrieked Sylvester,

"Yikes!"

leaping several feet into the air. "It's alive!"

"There's a vewy weal person under that wapping," said Tweety, "and I bet I know who!"

He grabbed a trailing piece of the mummy's cloth wrapping and started to unwind it, while Sylvester yowled for help.

"Can't let the others see me," Alaric mumbled. He dashed around a corner into another tunnel.

"He's getting away!" Tweety chirped. "Quick, Puddy Tat! You take this end of the bandage and

"He's Getting Away!"

hold him while I go find Gwanny and the guide!"

Tweety flew off in search of help, leaving Sylvester to play tug-of-war with the mummy.

Alaric Degoth pulled as hard as he could, trying to wrest the bandage from the tomcat's grasp. And around the corner, Sylvester tugged just as hard, trying to prevent the desperate mummy's escape.

Suddenly Alaric Degoth's foot slipped and he let go of the cloth. Feeling the pressure eased on the

A Tug-of-War

other side, Sylvester gave the cloth a tremendous yank.

Alaric Degoth spun madly as the long bandage unwrapped itself. Sylvester spun just as madly as the cloth wrapped itself around him.

The last of the bandage snapped free from Alaric, sending him crashing into a wall. Bells rang in his head, and bright stars twinkled before his eyes.

Still dazed and dizzy, he stumbled back into the passageway, where he saw Sylvester wrapped from head to toe in the bandage.

A Sudden Turn of Events

"Help!" he screamed. "It's a mummy! Hellllp!" He turned and ran to the tunnel's entrance, seeking only escape from the "mummy."

Just then, Tweety's voice sounded from the other end of the tunnel. "This way, Gwanny! Quick! I'm afwaid the mummy's got Sylvester!"

Tweety led Granny and the guide to the bandaged figure. "That's him!" he cried.

Granny beat the mummy with her handbag. "You evil thing!

"Help! It's a Mummy!"

What have you done with my pussycat?"

"Mmmmph! Glub!" mumbled Sylvester, clawing frantically at the bandages over his mouth. "It's me, Granny! Stop hitting me! The guy that was the mummy got away!"

Granny dropped her handbag and, with Tweety's help, began to unwrap Sylvester.

"I never saw anyone get into so much mischief!" she scolded as they finished the unwrapping. "Now, come along, boys. We have

"Granny! Stop Hitting Me!"

two more pyramids to visit before we leave!"

"Er, if you don't mind, Granny," said Sylvester, "I'm going back to the hotel. As far as I'm concerned, this tour is *all wrapped up!*"

"Come Along, Boys."

Watching TV

CHAPTER 9

SYLVESTER'S REVENGE

Tweety was watching TV in their room at a lodge in Canada when Sylvester came in and asked, "Where did Granny go?"

"On the cruise around Pine Lake." Tweety was watching his favorite program, *Lieutenant Beaky and His Balloononauts.*

Abruptly the cat's paw snatched him up, popped him into his cage, and locked the door. Then Sylvester raced outside with the cage. Deep in the surrounding woods, he hung the cage on a branch.

"What's the idea, Puddy Tat?" Tweety demanded, shaking the bars of the cage.

"Revenge!" cried Sylvester. "Pure, sweet revenge for the stunts you pulled on me during our trip! Now *you* can miss the fun for once! I'll bring you birdseed sandwiches from time to time." Triumphantly,

Sylvester's Revenge

Sylvester marched away.

"Poor Puddy has snapped at last," sighed Tweety. "All I did was twy to help him."

From behind a thick screen of trees came a distant wail—"Aauugh!"—followed by sudden silence.

"Uh-oh, I tawt I heard a Puddy Tat in twouble! Lucky I keep a couple of tools in here." Tweety got out a saw, rolled back the rug, and quickly cut a hole to freedom. He flew in the direction of Sylvester's outcry. Rounding a

Cutting a Hole

bush, he came upon a bound and gagged Sylvester!

The man bending over the cat saw Tweety. "Aha, here's the other one! If you don't want your pal hurt, little birdie, you'd better get me the Magic Voice quick!"

"Glub, glub!" said Sylvester behind his gag.

Tweety was astonished. "How do you know about the Magic Voice?"

"I've followed you around the world, trying to get it, ever since you won the singing contest. I let

Bound and Gagged

the cat out of his cage on the ship. I chased you in a balloon in France. I ruined your singing career in Venice. I led you to the dungeon in Scotland. In Portugal I had to save this stupid cat from killing himself, because the Voice would have been destroyed with him! I was the mummy in Egypt. Each time, something kept me from getting the Magic Voice. *I* stole the chemical from Professor Branepan, and it's *mine!* Now, here in Canada, I'll have it at last!"

"But why do you want it?" asked

"It's Mine!"

a bewildered Tweety.

"So I can have great power!" cried Alaric Degoth. "I will have it analyzed, and I—I alone!—will have the formula for making it. The chemical will make my orders so delightfully irresistible that everyone will want to do as I say. I will gain control of the country —of the entire world!"

Tweety thought, *What a cwackpot he is!*

The crackpot grabbed up Sylvester. "Get me the Voice, bird, or your friend loses all nine lives!"

A Serious Threat

Tweety's wings drooped as he nodded sadly. "All wight, Mr. Cwackpot, the Magic Voice is here." He flew to Sylvester and took the glass vial from the cat.

"Aha!" said Alaric, reaching.

"Catch!" called Tweety. He flung the glass vial toward a pile of rocks behind Alaric.

Clink, tinkle! The vial shattered into a hundred pieces as Alaric ran to catch it. *Poof, poof!* All the capsules disappeared in tiny clouds of vapor. Alaric sneezed and sneezed and sneezed.

"Catch!"

"Gone!" he cried. "Every single one—gone forever! Ow-ow!" He sank down and sobbed loudly, howling with grief. "Now I'll never rule the world. *Ow-ow-ow!*"

—Another howling answered him from the deep woods.

"Doodness, wolves!" said Tweety nervously as he scrambled on top of Sylvester. The cat wriggled helplessly in his bonds.

The wolf pack burst into the clearing and surrounded Alaric Degoth. He jumped up. "Help! Call them off!" He ran away into

Howling With Grief

the woods, yelling, with the wolves following closely, charmed by the sound of his voice.

Tweety wiped his forehead. "That was close! I'm glad we won't have any more twouble from him!"

"Glub, glub!" said Sylvester.

"Poor Puddy Tat, you want me to untie you?"

Sylvester nodded eagerly.

"Do you say pwetty please?"

Sylvester nodded and nodded.

Tweety persisted. "Do you say pwetty please with sugar on it?"

Nod, nod!

"That Was Close!"

"Let me think. Say please with sugar, and promise to do me a favor every week."

Tears of exasperation rolled down Sylvester's cheeks, but he nodded.

"Mmm," said Tweety. "How about pretty please, a favor each week, no chasing, and—"

But Sylvester had reached his limit. His face turned red as he swelled with rage. The bonds burst and he roared, "I'm gonna pull out every feather—one at a time!"

Tweety flew just out of reach of

Tweety Teases

his claws. *Now that our world tour is nearly over, it's nice to have Puddy Tat back to his normal mean, terrible, nasty self!* he thought. Then he flew off to find Granny who would, he knew, tell the mean, terrible, nasty Puddy Tat to behave himself.

An Angry Sylvester

Other **BIG LITTLE BOOKS**® Available

BATMAN—The Cheetah Caper

*__BUGS BUNNY__**—The Last Crusader

*__DONALD DUCK__**—The Lost Jungle City

THE FANTASTIC FOUR in the House of
Horrors

GRIMM'S GHOST STORIES

LASSIE—Old One-Eye

THE LONE RANGER Outwits Crazy Cougar

MICKEY MOUSE—Mystery at Disneyland

*__THE PINK PANTHER__**—Adventures in Z-Land

POPEYE—Danger, Ahoy!

SPIDER-MAN Zaps Mr. Zodiac

TWEETY AND SYLVESTER—The Magic Voice

*With "FLIP-IT" cartoons

WHITMAN® Classics

WHITMAN® *Mystery Adventures*

TRIXIE BELDEN